Text © 1992 Kirsten McKorkell
Illustration © 1992 Peter Kavanagh
Published exclusively for
Safeway
6 Millington Road, Hayes, Middx UB3 4AY
by Julia MacRae Books
a division of Random House
20 Vauxhall Bridge Road
London SW1V 2SA

First published 1992

Printed in Hong Kong

ISBN 1-85681-006-2

The *Christmas* MOUSE

Kirsten McCorkell and Peter Kavanagh

SAFEWAY SUPERBOOKS

It was Christmas Eve.

Everyone in the family was very busy.
Mum was in the kitchen making her extra-special
large mince pies.

Dad was in the dining room wrapping up
presents. No one was allowed to go in!

Kate and Penny were in the sitting room making
the stable for the Nativity Scene.

Millie Mouse was very interested in what
they were doing.

Penny had cut up a box and Kate had painted it.

ow they needed some hay to put in the manger
to make a bed for Baby Jesus.

   "Let's use some of Millie Mouse's hay,"
said Penny. "I'm sure she won't mind.
Be careful. We don't want Millie to escape . . ."

Too late!
Millie squeezed past Kate's
hand, ran down her arm and disappeared.

Mum and Dad came to help Kate and Penny catch Millie Mouse but it was no good. They couldn't see her,

not the tip of her tail, not even one whisker.
Millie had got clean away! Everyone looked for her.

"Cheer up," said Mum. "Let's put Mary and Joseph into the stable."

"But not Baby Jesus," said Penny. "Baby Jesus won't be born until Christmas Day."

Mum gave Kate and Penny some lemonade and an extra-specially large mince pie to leave on a tray for Father Christmas.

Millie was still missing at bedtime, and Kate and Penny felt very sad. Even the thought of Father Christmas and stockings didn't cheer them up.

But on Christmas morning, they rushed downstairs

to see if Father Christmas had eaten his mince pie.

"Oh," cried Penny. "He's eaten nearly all the mince pie. Look at the tiny toothmarks in it."

"Those can't be Father Christmas's nibbly little teeth," said Kate. "He's a big man with big teeth."

"LOOK!" cried Mum.

Mum lifted Millie carefully out of the manger. Millie's whiskers twitched a little but otherwise she didn't stir.

"I think there was too much mince pie for such a little mouse," said Mum.

Then Kate put Baby Jesus in the manger.
"Happy Christmas," she said, so softly that only
Baby Jesus would hear.